This book belongs to

Mrs. Shaun Brown

Thanks for being a wonderful Teacher! We Love You!

Chase

Carleigh

camrin with naza

Ashleigh Steinberg

Gabriella Esquivel

Juliet Vierie

Sophia Olaos

Sonali Shivali

Kevin Quallis

Meera Shanbhag

Abigail Disman :)

Katie Cullen

william Engle

Maddie Ulmer

Joey egert

Angela Lee (SnowWhite)

Megan Szostak

Ishaan (A. Chao)

Lauren Robinson

Lindsay Plotkin

Theresa Rivelle

Zoe Shapiro

Anna Hovet Hi :)

Craig Harvey

Kaitlyn Shaw

Julianna stegall

Erin Duncan

Walt Disney's

Snow White and the Seven Dwarfs

A Read-Aloud Storybook

Adapted by Liza Baker

MOUSE WORKS

Find us at www.DisneyBooks.com for more Mouse Works fun!

Illustrated by Atelier Philippe Harchy.
 For information, address Mouseworks, 114 Fifth Avenue, New York, New York 10011-5690.
Printed in the United States of America.
ISBN: 0-7364-0122-9

Magic Mirror on the Wall

Once upon a time, there lived a beautiful princess named Snow White. Her stepmother, the Queen, was jealous of Snow White's beauty.

Every day the Queen would ask, "Magic mirror on the wall, who is the fairest one of all?"

Each time the mirror would answer, "You are."

But one day the mirror replied, "A lovely maid I see, who is more fair than thee."

"It's Snow White!" snarled the Queen.

At that moment, Snow White was in the courtyard singing as she went about her chores.

A handsome young prince was riding by and heard her lovely voice. He climbed the castle wall to find her. Shy Snow White ran up to her balcony.

From the courtyard below, the Prince sang to Snow White. She listened happily to his song, and did not see the evil queen watching them.

Enraged with jealousy, the Queen ordered her huntsman, "Take Snow White into the forest and kill her."

The huntsman led Snow White deep into the woods, but he could not harm her. "I can't do as the Queen wishes!" he wept. "Run away, child, and never come back!"

Snow White fled into the forest. As she ran, she felt haunting eyes watching her. The trees seemed to reach out to grab her.

With nowhere left to run, she fell to the ground and began to cry.

In the midst of her tears, Snow White looked up and found herself surrounded by forest animals. "Do you know where I can stay?" she asked them.

The friendly animals led Snow White to a tiny cottage in the woods.

"It's like a doll's house!" said Snow White. She knocked at the door but no one answered. "May I come in?" she called. Slowly she stepped inside.

As Snow White wandered through the house she discovered seven little chairs and seven little beds.

"Seven little children must live here! Let's clean the house and surprise them," the Princess suggested. "Then maybe they'll let me stay."

The Seven Dwarfs

Close by, the seven dwarfs who owned the cottage were busy working in their mine. All day long they dug for jewels.

At five o'clock it was time to go. Doc led Grumpy, Happy, Sleepy, Sneezy, Bashful, and Dopey home, singing and whistling as they went.

When the dwarfs reached their cottage the light was on—someone was in their house! They crept inside and tiptoed upstairs to find Snow White fast asleep beneath their blankets.

"It's a monster!" whispered one dwarf.

Stepping closer, Doc cried out, "Why, it's a girl!"

Snow White sat up and said, "How do you do?"

She explained to the dwarfs who she was and what the evil queen had planned for her. "Don't send me away," she begged.

“If you let me stay, I’ll wash and sew and sweep and cook,” Snow White promised.

At that the dwarfs shouted, “Hooray! She stays!” And the happy princess ran to the kitchen to prepare dinner.

The dwarfs rushed downstairs to eat, but Snow White said, "Supper is not quite ready. You'll just have time to wash."

"Wash?" cried the bewildered dwarfs.

All the dwarfs but one headed to the tub. "I'd like to see anybody make *me* wash!" said Grumpy.

Just as Grumpy spoke, the other dwarfs pounced on him and dumped him into the tub. They scrubbed him squeaky-clean. "You'll pay for this!" growled Grumpy.

Back at the castle, the Queen asked the mirror once again, "Who is the fairest in the land?"

"Snow White," answered the mirror. Then it revealed where the Princess was hiding.

The angry Queen drank a potion that disguised her as an old hag. Then she created a magic apple. "With one bite of this poisoned apple, Snow White's eyes will close forever," she cackled. The only cure for the sleeping spell was love's first kiss.

Unaware of the Queen's plot,
Snow White and the Seven Dwarfs
sang and danced late into the night.

The next morning, Snow White kissed each dwarf good-bye as he marched off toward the mine.

Doc warned the Princess, "The Queen is a sly one. Beware of strangers!"

The Sleeping Spell

From the shadows of the trees, the Queen watched the dwarfs leave. Slowly, she crept up to the cottage.

"All alone, my pet?" the disguised queen asked Snow White. Then she offered the poisoned apple. "Go on, dearie. Have a bite."

Several birds recognized the wicked queen and knocked the apple from her hands. But Snow White felt sorry for the old woman and helped her inside the cottage.

Sensing danger, the forest animals ran off to warn the dwarfs. But it was too late.

Snow White bit into the poisoned fruit!

Dropping the apple, Snow White fell to the ground. "Now I'll be the fairest in the land!" cackled the Queen.

Lightning flashed and thunder cracked as the Queen fled from the cottage.

But before she could escape, the Seven Dwarfs came charging at her.

"There she goes," cried Grumpy. "After her!"

The dwarfs chased the Queen to the top of a rocky cliff.

"I'll fix you!" she shrieked as she tried to roll an enormous boulder down on top of them.

Suddenly, a bolt of lighting struck the ledge where the Queen stood!

The rock crumbled beneath her feet and the evil queen tumbled off the mountaintop and into the darkness below.

The heartbroken dwarfs built a coffin for Snow White and watched over her day and night. Then one day the Prince appeared.

The Prince had searched far and wide for the beautiful princess.

With great sorrow, he kissed Snow White farewell.

Slowly, Snow White began to awaken. The Prince's kiss had broken the spell! The dwarfs cheered and hugged one another joyously.

Snow White thanked the dwarfs for all they had done, then kissed each one good-bye. Together, the Prince and Snow White rode off to his castle, where they lived happily ever after.